A First Flight® Level Three Reader

Matthew *and the* Midnight Wrestlers

By Allen Morgan

Illustrated by
Michael Martchenko

Fitzhenry & Whiteside

Published in Canada by Fitzhenry & Whiteside,
195 Allstate Parkway, Markham, Ontario L3R 4T8

Published in the United States by Fitzhenry & Whiteside,
311 Washington Street, Brighton, Massachusetts 02135

www.fitzhenry.ca godwit@fitzhenry.ca

10 9 8 7 6 5 4 3 2 1

Library and Archives Canada Cataloguing in Publication

Morgan, Allen, 1946-
Matthew and the midnight wrestlers / Allen Morgan ;
illustrated by Micheal Martchenko.

Originally published: Toronto: Stoddart, 1998.
[40] p. : col. ill. ; cm.
Summary: The neighborhood bully picks on Matthew after art classes,
but at midnight Matthew teams up with artist/wrestler Tooloose the Wrecker
to face off against his foe in the ultimate wrestling and painting match.
ISBN 1-55041-915-3
ISBN 1-55041-916-1 (pbk.)

1. Pirates – Fiction — Juvenile literature. 2. Wrestlers– Fiction – Juvenile literature.
3. Artists – Fiction — Juvenile literature. I. Martchenko , Michael. I. Title.
[E] dc22   PZ7.M674Mmw 2005

PS8576.O642M38 2005   jC813'.54   C2005-905857-9

**U.S. Publisher Cataloging-in-Publication Data
(Library of Congress Standards)**

Fitzhenry & Whiteside acknowledges with thanks the Canada Council for the Arts,
and the Ontario Arts Council for their support of our publishing program.
We acknowledge the financial support of the Government of Canada
through the Book Publishing Industry Development Program (BPIDP)
for our publishing activities.

Design by Wycliffe Smith Design Inc
Printed in Hong Kong

For Merlin

A.M.

To the newest member of the family,
Alexander Jacques Martin

M.M.

CHAPTER ONE

One Saturday, when Matthew was walking home from his art class, he saw Big Mike waiting for him just outside the house.

Matthew made a dash for the door, but he tripped and fell before he was halfway there.

Big Mike stomped over. "Where are you going?" he growled.

Matthew knew there might be trouble, but luckily his mother called from inside the house. "Matthew! It's time for lunch!"

When Big Mike heard Matthew's mother, he didn't want to stay.

"I'll see you later on," he said, as he walked away.

After lunch Matthew decided to watch some TV while he worked on his art. Wrestling was on. One of the tag teams was dressed up as artists. It got Matthew thinking. To see how it looked, he drew himself bigger with lots of muscles.

He was sketching a flashy red cape when his mother brought him a glass of milk.

"You forgot to drink this at lunch," she said.

CHAPTER TWO

Later on, when it was time for bed, Matthew's mother tucked him in. "Was that boy giving you trouble today?" she asked.

"Maybe a little," Matthew admitted.

"Keep drinking your milk," his mother said. "You'll grow big and strong, and before very long you'll be just as big as he is."

She kissed him goodnight and turned out the light.

Matthew wasn't sure that milk alone

would do the trick. "If I were strong and I had a good costume, I could take care of Big Mike—no problem," he told himself as he fell asleep.

At the stroke of midnight, Matthew woke up. He heard some slapping sounds in the street, so he went outside. A man was jumping rope.

"Want to wrestle?" the man asked Matthew. "I'm one guy short for a tag-team match. You do any special stuff?"

"I run pretty fast and I like to draw."

"Good enough. Let's make the shake. My name's Taloose: Taloose the Wrecker."

"They call me Matthew."

"That's it, kid? That'll never fly. When you're in the wrestling game, the name is half the thing. You say you're fast? We'll call you Dash. Slap Dash the Masher!"

A few moments later a horse arrived, pulling a wagon.

"Dash, this is Harry: Harry the Horse. Harry meet Slap Dash the Masher!"

The horse looked Matthew up and down then shook his head. "The kid couldn't mash a potato," he said.

"He's not going to cook; he's going to wrestle. He says he runs fast. Let's see if he can!"

So Matthew ran around the block.

Even the horse was impressed. "Let's hitch him up to the wagon," he said.

15

CHAPTER THREE

When they got to the Wrestling Gallery,
Taloose grabbed paper and pens.

"To help the referee score the fight,
draw a picture of something you like. You
get points for wrestling and points for
art. You've got to do both to win," he said.

Matthew drew his mother the way
she looked when she woke up each morn-
ing.

"Not bad," said Taloose. "She's got
that killer look in her eye, the same as
you do, kid."

16

18

"I'm not really sure I'm strong enough to be a wrestler," Matthew said.

"No problem, kid. I've got just the thing," Taloose assured him. "Try some of this. I make it myself. It helps you get strong really fast."

It looked a lot like milk when Taloose poured it out. But the masking-tape label on the side of the carton said Wrestler's Juice, so Matthew drank the whole glass.

20

Chapter Four

At the wrestling ring, the referee announced, "In this corner: Madman Magritte with his Hat of Horror! Dangerous Dali, and Pablo Diablo! And that pervasive purveyor of bad behavior, the Masked Marvel!"

"They look pretty dangerous," Matthew whispered.

"We can take them," Taloose replied.

"And in this corner: Lawnmower Harris, Murderer Moore, and Taloose the Wrecker! And in his first professional bout—he's fast, he's bold, he's not very old—Slap Dash the Masher!

The bell rang and the fight began. The crowd went wild! So did the wrestlers. They fought in the ring and they battled in the seats. Even the fans got involved.

24

By the end of Round One, most of the wrestlers were knocked out cold.

"It's just you and me," Taloose told Matthew as they chugged a few slugs of Wrestler's Juice. "I'll fight Dali. You take the Marvel."

"He looks kind of familiar," Matthew said.

"Take off his mask if you get a chance," Taloose advised. "And be sure to watch out for his favorite move— it's called the atomic body slam."

CHAPTER FIVE

Round Two began. Dangerous Dali was disqualified for putting ants down Taloose's pants. Taloose got the wiggles so he was gone, too. It was all up to Matthew now! But just when it looked like he might win the day, he tripped on his cape. The Masked Marvel climbed to the top of the corner post.

"Your mom can't help you now," he growled. Then he jumped.

WHAM! The Masked Marvel landed his body slam move. But Matthew rolled to the side just in time, so the Masked Marvel slammed himself senseless instead. Matthew reached over and pulled off his mask.

"Big Mike!" he cried.

The final bell rang and the fight was done. The score was tied for the wrestling; but when they compared Matthew's picture to Mike's, there was no doubt about which team had won.

CHAPTER SIX

When they went out to the street again, Taloose had some work to do.

"I've got a lot of deliveries to make," he told Matthew. "You want to help?"

Matthew did. So they drove around for an hour or two, dropping off cartons of Wrestler's Juice to all the artists in town.

When they were through, Taloose and Harry brought Matthew home.

"You keep my share of the wrestling prize," Matthew told Taloose. "I need to buy some of your Wrestler's Juice."

"You got it, kid," Taloose replied, and he handed Matthew a carton. "I'll drop off a new one every week. It'll make you strong—as strong as a horse and twice as wary, too."

"Works for me!" agreed Harry.

Matthew felt a little bit sleepy, so he said goodnight and went inside. He put the Wrestler's Juice in the fridge and climbed the stairs to his room. Soon he was fast asleep.

CHAPTER SEVEN

At six o'clock Matthew woke up. He ran into his mother's room.

"Wake up and guess who I am!" he cried.

His mother seemed to need a few clues, so Matthew explained about wrestling and art.

"Slap Dash the Masher's my wrestling name!" Matthew exclaimed.

Then he showed his mother the wrestling moves he'd learned from

Taloose. They worked very well, at least for a while. But then his mother discovered she knew a few moves of her own. She subdued Matthew in two seconds flat with the Super Mom Tickle Hold.

In the kitchen, Matthew's mother opened the fridge. "That's funny," she said. "There's masking tape on the milk."

"It isn't milk," Matthew explained. "It's Wrestler's Juice. I got it from Taloose."

"Mat, I've been thinking. Maybe you'd like to take judo lessons. You can go on Saturday after your art class."

"That sounds okay," Matthew agreed. "And you know what, Mom? You've got some good moves. I bet you could be on a tag team, too. All you need is a wrestling name. How about King Kong the Killer Mom?"

"I think I'd rather be Tickler's Mother," she said as she moved toward him.

"We'll practice stuff like that later on," Matthew explained as he jumped out of the way. "Right now it's time for training, Mom. Do you want a glass of my Wrestler's Juice?"

"No thanks, dear," his mother said. "I already have my very own special brew of Wrestler's Juice."

FIRST FLIGHT®

FIRST FLIGHT READERS

Featuring award-winning authors and illustrators and a fabulous cast of characters, First Flight readers introduce children to the joy of reading.

Short stories with simple sentences and recognizable words for children eager to read. Ideal for sharing with your emergent reader.

High interest stories and language play for developing readers. Slightly longer sentences and words may require a little help.

More complex themes and plots for the independent reader. These stories have short chapters with lively illustrations on each page.

Much longer chapters with black line illustrations interspersed throughout the book for confident, independent readers.